CHOOSE YOUR OWN ADVENTURE®

Your Very Own ROBOT Goes Cuckoo-Bananas!

R. A. MONTGOMERY & SHANNON GILLIGAN

A DRAGONLARK BOOK

A DRAGONLARK BOOK

CHOOSE YOUR OWN ADVENTURE®

Kids Love Reading
Choose Your Own Adventure®!

"If you think kidnapping, money, and
adventure are exciting, read it!"
Logan Wilson, age 7

"It was a good book."
Gabriel Frankel, age 8

"If you don't read this book, you'll get payback."
Amy Cook, age 8 ½

"I thought this book was funny.
I think younger and older kids will like it."
Tessa Jernigan, age 6 ½

"This is fun reading. Once you go in to have an
adventure, you may never come out."
Jude Fidel, age 7

Illustrated by: Keith Newton
Book design: Stacey Boyd, Big Eyedea Visual Design
For information regarding permission, write to:

CHOOSECO
P.O. Box 46
Waitsfield, Vermont 05673
www.cyoa.com

A DRAGONLARK BOOK

ISBN: 1-933390-39-5
EAN: 978-1-933390-39-0

Published simultaneously in the United States and Canada

Printed in China.

13 12 11 10 9 8 7 6 5 4

"Sweetheart, I have to go next door for five minutes," your mom says. "Can you and Gus stay out of trouble while I'm gone?"

"Yes, Mom," you reply. "I promise."

"You remember what your father and I said?" she asks.

"Yes. If Gus gets into trouble one more time..."

"...he's going back where he came from," your mother says, finishing your sentence.

Gus is a robot. Your very own robot. You made him last summer from spare parts you found in the trash can in your parents' lab. "Going back where he came from" means one thing for Gus. It means getting thrown out in the garbage.

Turn to the next page.

"Your Dad and I are serious," she adds, as if you need reminding.

"I know," you answer. "We'll be good."

Your mom waves as she heads out the back door. You look over at Gus, who gives you a wink.

This is not a good sign.

"I don't get it. Why is your mom so mad?" Gus says as soon as your mom is gone.

Turn to page 4.

3

"Well, there was the time you flooded the basement so you could play submarine," you say.

"But the bathtub wasn't big enough!" Gus cries.

"And then the time you cut down the apple trees out back to build a fort," you remind him.

"Those apple trees were getting old anyway," Gus answers. "Plus, even your mom said it opened up the view."

"What about the time you turned the kitchen into a fast-food restaurant for wandering robots?" you ask.

"Yeah, you're probably right about that one," Gus says. "But listen. I've got an idea."

"What kind of idea? Will it get us in trouble?" you ask.

Turn to page 7.

TRIING! TRIING!

Gus jerks his head to the right. It's the phone ringing. And Gus loves the phone almost as much as pizza with pineapple.

"Please can I answer?" he begs.

"No, Gus," you reply. "Every time you use the phone, something bad happens."

You snatch the cell phone before Gus has the chance.

"Hello?" you say into the mouthpiece.

Before the caller says a thing, Gus goes into robot twirling mode.

Uh-oh.

Sparks shoot out like the 4th of July, a loud ZZZZZZzzzz pierces the air, and purple smoke puffs out of his transistor ears and microphone mouth.

With a burst of energy, Gus lifts off, spins sixteen times in less than one second and VANISHES!

Turn to page 8.

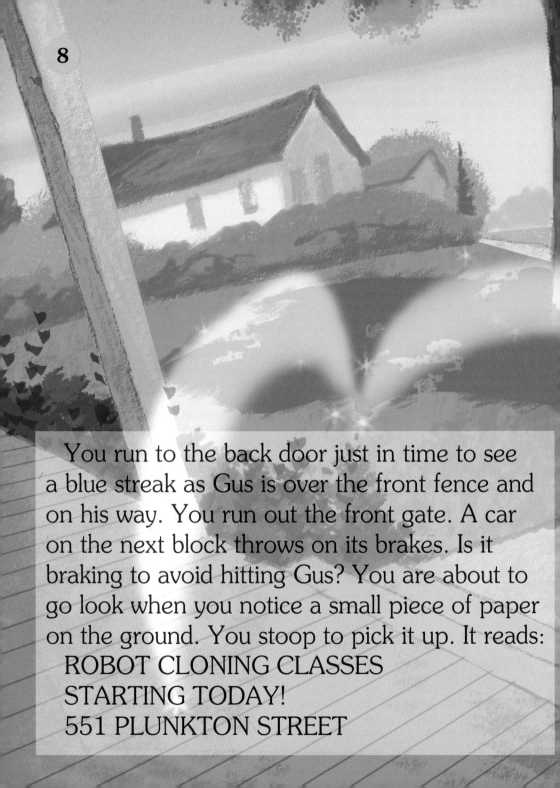

You run to the back door just in time to see a blue streak as Gus is over the front fence and on his way. You run out the front gate. A car on the next block throws on its brakes. Is it braking to avoid hitting Gus? You are about to go look when you notice a small piece of paper on the ground. You stoop to pick it up. It reads:
ROBOT CLONING CLASSES
STARTING TODAY!
551 PLUNKTON STREET

You groan. Gus wants to clone himself? Make more robots just like Gus? He's headed to the trash heap now for sure! You have to save Gus. But what can you do?

If you run toward the sound of the braking car, hoping it's Gus, turn to page 10.

If you decide to go to the Robot Cloning classes to find Gus, turn to page 13.

You decide to run toward the braking sound. A car is turning right at the next corner. Otherwise the street is empty.

"Gus?" you holler.

But it's silent. The only noise is the sprinkler going off at the house across from you.

Suddenly a brick lands at your feet. Thwack! It has a message attached to it with some twine: GET ALL THE MONEY IN YOUR PIGGY BANK. MEET ME AT THE SEWAGE TREATMENT PLANT. TELL NO ONE. REPEAT, NO ONE!!

Go on to the next page.

The sewage treatment plant? You get a sinking feeling. The sewage treatment plant has a special new computer. It was on the news last night. You noticed that Gus paid close attention. Gus loves everything about computers.

You have to act fast. Should you run back home, get your money and bike to the sewage treatment plant? Or should you choose the extreme option and find your friend Schuyler? You don't like Schuyler much lately. She's gotten really bossy. But Gus has a big crush on her. He'll do whatever she says.

Turn to page 12.

If you decide to run home, get your money stash and sneak off to the sewage plant alone, turn to page 18.

If you decide to go to Schuyler for help, turn to page 25.

You decide to walk to 551 Plunkton Street. A sign on the door says "Robot Cloning Class in Session—2nd Floor."

When you get there, the first robot you see is Gus.

"Gus!" you exclaim. "What are you doing here?"

"I'm not Gus," the robot replies. "Not the original Gus anyway. I'm Gus 6."

"Uh, what do you mean Gus 6?"

"I was cloned from Gus the original last week," Gus 6 replies.

"Last WEEK?" you cry.

"Sure. We all were," Gus 6 adds.

Turn to the next page.

He sweeps his Gus-identical arm around the room. "There's Gus 3, and that one with the green star on his shoulder is Gus 7. There's Gus 11, 13 and 9. And…"

Everywhere you look you see Gus. You start to feel dizzy. The room begins to tilt.

"Are you okay?" another Gus asks, stepping forward.

Before you can answer, everything fades to black.

Turn to page 16.

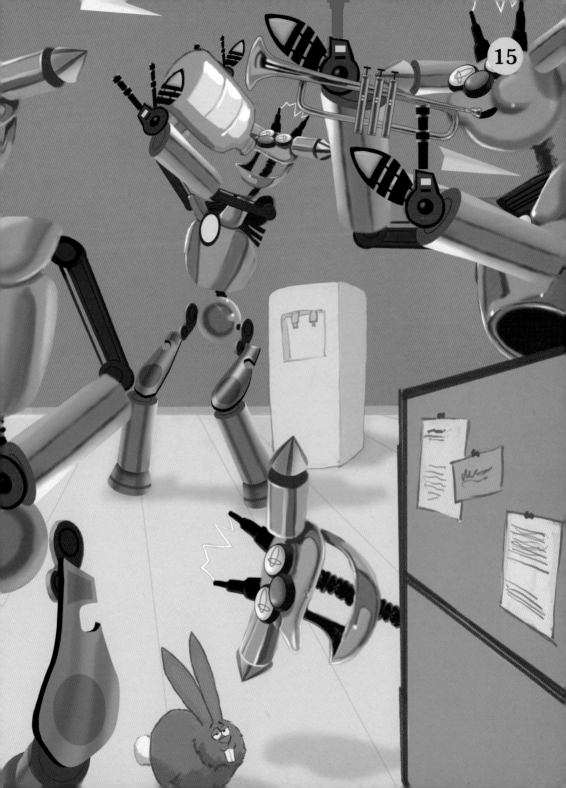

"Honey? Are you okay? It's me, Mom."

You open your eyes. You're back at home, lying in bed.

"Mom, I had this terrible dream," you say. "I dreamed Gus cloned himself. There were Guses everywhere."

"You weren't dreaming, sweetheart," your mom replies. She strokes your cheek. "Gus *did* clone himself. Without permission, of course."

"Gus never asks permission!" you cry.

Your mom smiles wisely.

"But the good news is that we think we can sell the Gus clones," she adds. "And we'll put the profits in your piggy bank."

There's a knock at the door, and Gus sticks his head inside your room.

"And then we'll use the money for a trip to outer space!" he exclaims.

The End

"Cousin?" you ask. "Gus doesn't have a cousin. I built him from scratch myself."

"It's just a figure of speech. We possess identical motherboards," the robot answers. "My name is Lizzie. I work here in computers. Gus is quite smart. He's found a problem with our new computer. I think he caught it just in time."

You follow Lizzie up the hall. She knocks on a door marked *Hazard—Stay Out*. It opens, and you both march inside.

Turn to page 53.

You decide to go straight home for some money and your bike. It will be fastest. And Gus gets into trouble faster than anyone you know.

You turn around and start to run. Two doors from your house, you trip on something. Was it a wire? You go flying through the air, and land on the sidewalk with a loud THWAACK!

"Ow!" you yelp.

"What's the matter, pipsqueak?" a nasty voice says. "Can't even run right?"

You look up to see two familiar size 12 sneakers three inches from your nose.

Go on to the next page.

They belong to Harry Hill, the biggest bully in school. Someone snickers in the bushes. It must be Harry's best pal, Nathan. Nathan is busily winding a spool of wire. You were tripped on purpose.

"Get up, pipsqueak!" Harry bellows. "Now!"

If you decide to jump up and make a run for it, turn to page 23.

If you decide to stay and face down Harry and Nathan, turn to page 32.

"There are only three places Gus could have gotten into the big pipes," Schuyler says, pointing to the plans. "Here, here or here."

"Which one is closest to the computer room?" you ask. "I think that is where he was headed."

"Here." Schuyler points to the map. "But this entrance is pretty close too," she adds.

"How do we get there from here?" you ask.

"I know a secret route through the basement. I used to come out here with my dad on weekends when they were building the place. Follow me."

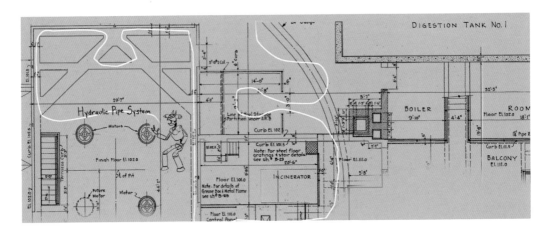

Turn to page 65.

Schuyler makes you so mad, you can practically feel the steam coming out your ears.

"Gus is fine," you shrug. "I just came by to say hi. But I can see you're in one of your bad moods. See you around."

You wave goodbye like you couldn't care less, take three porch steps in one jump, and take off. You'd rather face Gus on your own than have to be nice to Schuyler.

Turn to page 28.

Harry isn't as fast as he looks. Maybe you can make it into your yard before he gets you. You stand up slowly, brushing yourself off casually.

"What's that?" you say curiously, pointing to the phone pole across the street.

When Harry and Nathan turn to look, you make your move. But you're not fast enough. Harry Hill tackles you. The two of you fall into the bushes wrestling. Harry starts to throw punches. Thanks to your speed, they mostly miss.

"Help!" you yell. "Gus! Help me! GUS!!!"

An ear-splitting whistle fills the air. It's coming closer. Harry stops punching you to look up.

Something streaks by, trailed by a wisp of blue smoke. It turns around and streaks back. Harry Hill tries to duck, but it's too late. The blue streak circles him a dozen times. He yells out like a baby.

"Stop! Stop that! Ouch! It hurts! Help!"

The blue streak ties up Harry Hill like a sausage. It's Gus!

Turn to page 30.

You decide to go to Schuyler's house. When you reach her back-porch stairs, she's already standing there. It's like she's been waiting for you.

"What is it now?" Schuyler sneers. "More robot trouble?"

She has her hand on her hip like she's really important. You notice she has grown another inch.

Sometimes you can't stand Schuyler.

If you tell Schuyler that Gus is doing fine, and leave to find your very own robot by yourself, turn to page 21.

If you tell Schuyler the truth about Gus and ask for her help, even if she is a huge pest, turn to page 48.

26

"I think Gus would use the entrance nearest to the computer," you whisper.

"I agree," Schuyler nods. "Follow me."

First you run down a long hall, then you sprint across a big room. Schuyler motions you to stop. She holds her finger to her lips and peeks around the corner.

"Okay," she says. "Let's go. We have to be fast."

The two of you round the corner. Before you get very far, you hear the sound of shouting. And lots of running feet. Suddenly a pack of people appear. They're coming straight at you. And Gus is in the lead.

"RUN!" he yells, streaking past.

"Wait!" you cry, turning around to run after Gus. "You're going too fast!"

"Gus, we can't keep up!" Schuyler yells.

"Grab my feet, quick!" Gus yells back.

"Your feet?" you cry.

Go on to the next page.

You look back. A pack of angry security guards and plant employees is gaining. You look forward. Gus is shooting off blue sparks, like he always does before going airborne.

"It's not the time to ask questions!" Gus shouts, as his feet begin to lift off the ground.

Turn to page 62.

The sewage treatment plant is not too far. You run the rest of the way. You know you are there when you come to the long chain-link fence that goes on forever. The fence surrounds the plant. And now it has a big robot-shaped hole in it.

The hole is right under a sign that says "STAY OUT DANGER."

If you ignore the sign and go in after Gus through the hole in the fence, turn to page 37.

If you decide to do things the normal, non-robot way and go to the front entrance of the sewage treatment plant, turn to page 50.

STAY OUT
DANGER

29

"Chew on that for a while," Gus tells Harry, coming to a stop.

"Gus!" you cry. "You saved me!"

You jump up and hug your robot.

"That's what a good robot is for," Gus announces.

"And a best friend," you add.

Go on to the next page.

"Wait!" Harry Hill yells as the two of you start to walk home. "Take me down. Right now! You can't leave me like this!"

"Wanna bet?" you ask, staring at his angry red face.

The End

You decide to stand up to Harry and Nathan. You get up as if nothing happened and continue home.

"Excuse me," you say, when Harry stands in your way.

"Where's your dumb robot?" Harry demands.

"He couldn't be here," you reply pleasantly. "He smells you a mile off."

This answer seems to make Harry mad. He lunges forward and gives you a big shove. You struggle to keep on your feet.

Go on to the next page.

You hear another pfffting sound, and a SNAP!

"OW!" Harry yells. He grabs the side of his neck.

This time the small pebble hits his ear. Harry yells again and spins around.

Turn to page 35.

All three of you turn to look in the direction of the pebble.

It's your neighbor, Mrs. Kathan! She's standing on her porch with a slingshot.

She lets off another one. This time Harry ducks.

"No one likes a bully, Harry Hill!" she hollers. "You get out of my neighborhood and don't come back."

Mrs. Kathan cues up another pebble.

Harry and Nathan exchange a look. And take off running.

"Thanks, Mrs. Kathan," you say cheerfully.

"Anytime," she says with a big smile.

She stows the slingshot in her sweater pocket and slowly walks back inside.

Wait till your parents and Gus hear this one!

The End

You dive through the hole in the chain-link fence. It catches and rips your t-shirt but you don't care. You've got to find Gus before he does something stupid.

Inside the fence, there is a stack of four huge pipes. Each of them is as big as you are. They could fit a whole person inside standing up.

There is a sign on one of them. It has an arrow pointing left that says "Main Building." Another arrow points to the right and says "Processing."

Where did Gus go? The new computer is probably in the Main Building. But Gus doesn't ever do the obvious.

If you go left and head to the Main Building to find Gus, turn to page 38.

If you take the path to the right and head toward Processing instead, turn to page 54.

You decide to follow the sign that points to the Main Building. You just know in your bones that Gus is after that new computer. The computer manages water flow and sewage for the whole city.

You enter the Main Building through a back door. It opens into a long hallway of offices. All the doors are closed.

Suddenly you hear voices. Someone is coming! You look around, but you don't have many options. What should you do?

If you decide to run up the hallway and away from the voices, turn to page 45.

If you stay where you are and pretend to be lost if anyone asks, turn to page 40.

Don't
Come
In
Here!

SERIOUS
OFFICE

No
Computer
In Here
Kid!

You freeze. The voices get closer. They round the corner.

"Gus!" you cry.

Your robot is walking between two men. He jerks at the sound of your voice. And gives you a friendly wave.

"There you are! I'm in trouble again," Gus says cheerfully. "But it's these two who are going to be in trouble soon."

"Gus!" you exclaim. "You can't talk like that to…to…strangers."

"Sure I can," Gus replies. "Especially when they are as stupid as these two."

You can't help but gasp.

"They've got the new computer programmed incorrectly," Gus states. "If they don't modify the sluicing algorithm, the whole enchilada is going to get backed up and blow sky-high."

The two men roll their eyes.

One of them asks, "Does he ever shut up?"

Go on to the next page.

You're about to say no, and he's rarely wrong either. But you decide one talker is enough.

Turn to page 42.

The two men take you to an office and tell you to wait while they call your mother. They lock the door behind them.

"Gus, we are really in for it," you moan.

"No, they are," states Gus. "I'm telling the truth. This whole place is about to blow. Does that window open? We've got to get out of here."

Somewhere deep inside the building, you hear a low rumble. Gus goes over and fiddles with the window next to the desk. He pushes it open.

"Follow me, O fearless leader," he says. Then he hops outside.

"Very funny," you say. You don't have a choice. You hop out the window too. If you leave Gus alone, who knows what kind of trouble he'll get in?

You walk alongside Gus for twenty minutes. Suddenly there's a loud BOOM!

"Thar she blows!" Gus shouts, as you watch a geyser of sewage shoot into the sky.

The End

The voices are coming closer. You decide to run up the hall in the other direction.

You run as quietly and quickly as you can. At the end of the hallway, it turns left. You run around the corner and run smack into…

"SCHUYLER!" you cry.

Schuyler jumps three feet and screams in surprise.

"What are you doing here?" you demand. "Did you follow me?"

"No, I didn't follow you," Schuyler says snottily. "I figured out where you were going when the phone rang right after you left. It was my dad. He said that there was a runaway robot in the sewage treatment plant. They needed the plans."

"The plans?" you ask.

Turn to the next page.

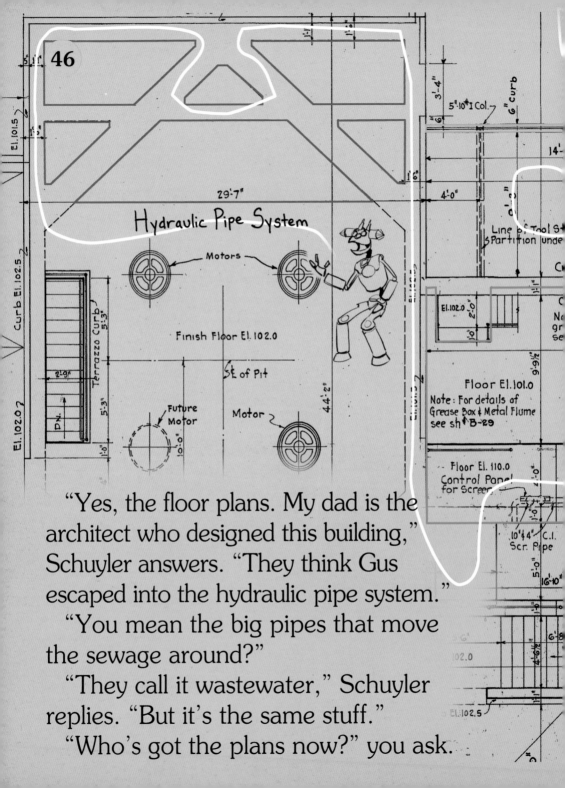

Hydraulic Pipe System

Motors

Finish Floor El. 102.0

℄ of Pit

Future Motor

Motor

"Yes, the floor plans. My dad is the architect who designed this building," Schuyler answers. "They think Gus escaped into the hydraulic pipe system."

"You mean the big pipes that move the sewage around?"

"They call it wastewater," Schuyler replies. "But it's the same stuff."

"Who's got the plans now?" you ask.

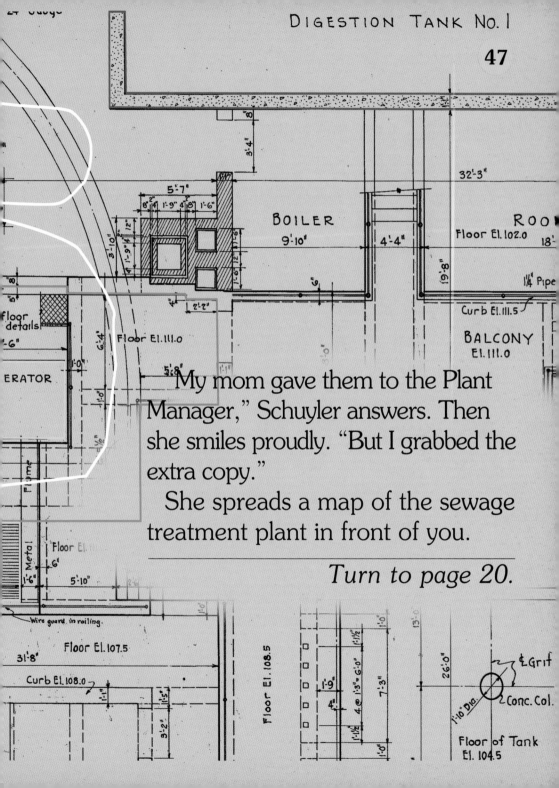

BOILER
9'-10"

ROO

Floor El. 102.0

18'-

1¼" Pipe

Curb El. 111.5

BALCONY
El. 111.0

floor
details

ERATOR

Floor El. 111.0

Floor El.

My mom gave them to the Plant Manager," Schuyler answers. Then she smiles proudly. "But I grabbed the extra copy."

She spreads a map of the sewage treatment plant in front of you.

Turn to page 20.

Wire guard in railing.

Floor El. 107.5

31'-8"

Curb El. 108.0

Floor El. 108.5

Floor of Tank
El. 104.5

℄ Grit

Conc. Col.

"Schuyler, Gus has disappeared," you say. "I think he took off for the sewage treatment plant. And if he gets into any more trouble…"

Schuyler suddenly perks up as if Gus getting into trouble has made her day.

"The sewage treatment plant?" she asks. "Follow me. I know a shortcut."

She jumps down all three back steps at once and heads into the woods across the road. You run after her onto a path you've never seen before. You huff and puff to keep up.

"How do you know about this?" you ask.

"I used to come out here all the time when my dad was designing it," she answers.

You arrive at the sewage plant from the rear. Schuyler slips through a hole in the chain link fence at the edge of the woods and stops.

"Do you have any idea where he was headed?" she asks.

"The new computer room, I think," you reply.

Go on to the next page.

Schuyler squints, thinking.

"Okay. We'll use the back door right here. And then go downstairs through the basement to the other side. That way no one will see us," she says.

You trot after Schuyler down a hill and enter the sewage treatment plant through the back door. It takes a minute for your eyes to get used to the dark.

"Okay, follow me."

Turn to page 65.

You decide to use the front entrance to the plant. You need to set a good example for Gus. If you jump through the robot-shaped hole, he'll notice right away. He'll say, "You broke the rules, and so can I!"

You reach the main building just as a tour of the new sewage plant is starting.

"Welcome to the most advanced wastewater treatment system in the state," the tour guide says proudly. "Please follow me and stay together."

You fall into step with the group, keeping your eyes peeled for Gus.

"The first stage of processing is grit removal," the guide explains. You are standing in a two-story hall filled with four huge metal tanks.

"Each of these tanks contains a filter bed," he adds, "to take out grit, sand, tin cans—you name it."

Turn to page 52.

While he continues talking, you crane your neck to look around. But there's no sign of Gus in Grit Removal. You just hope you find him before he gets into trouble. You wonder if your mom and dad really would throw him out. He's your masterpiece, after all.

Just then the guide announces, "Next stop is Ion Exchange."

Your tour group walks down a wide hall. As you pass by a pair of glass doors, you catch a glimpse of Gus! He's walking the other way and reading some papers. As your tour group disappears around the next corner, you open the glass door and slip inside.

"Gus!" you say in a loud whisper. But he just keeps walking. "Gus!" you repeat.

He turns around. But it's not Gus!

"I think you're looking for my cousin," the robot says.

Turn to page 17.

Gus is seated at a terminal and is typing on the keyboard like a maniac. Two more robots and an adult human stand behind him.

"Aren't you glad you let him give it a try?" one of the robots asks the human. The human's nametag says "Chief Engineer."

The engineer strokes his beard, and shakes his head. "It was those membrane ratio algorithms. I'll be darned. We could have blown up, if it weren't for your friend here."

Gus turns to give you a big wink. "I was wondering where you were."

The End

You decide to take a right to "Processing."

You walk alongside the four pipes. They bend left. When you turn the corner, six huge greenhouses come into view. They are all filled with plants. Greenhouses?

Just then someone behind you shouts "Stop! Right where you are!"

You whirl around. A security guard is marching toward you.

"I'm looking for my robot," you cry.

"Your what?" the man growls. "Quit being a wise-acre. You're trespassing."

"I do have a robot. I made him myself. His name is Gus. He escaped and I think he came here."

"Gus?" the man replies. "What a cute name for a robot. You can tell that to the nice police-man at the station."

"The police?" you croak.

Turn to page 56.

Minutes later you are sitting in the back seat of a security car, headed to the police station.

You try to tell the guard about all the bad things Gus has done.

"He once stole my mom's credit card and tried to buy a tractor," you say. "And then there was the time he pushed the emergency button in the elevator on a tour of the White House, and the Secret Service nearly arrested us."

You hope this scares him. But the guard just keeps saying, "Sure, kid, whatever."

There's nothing more you can do.

Gus is going to pay for this big time.

Turn to page 58.

Down at the police station, a nice police-woman listens to your story. Suddenly the intercom on her desk squawks.

"Emergency, Code 1. An explosion just reported on city property. All active duty officers please report to the Sewage Treatment Center at 2300 Circle Drive immediately. No injuries reported, but there's sewage every-where."

The policewoman gives you a good look.

"I tried to warn you. Gus always gets into trouble," you say. "It's his specialty."

Turn to page 60.

Another policeman runs into the room.

"Grab the kid," he orders, "and follow me. We're going to the sewage treatment plant. They just called. Something about a robot gone cuckoo bananas."

"That would be Gus, my very own robot!" you cry, jumping to your feet.

The policewoman eyes the security guard. "You should have listened to the kid," she says.

The End

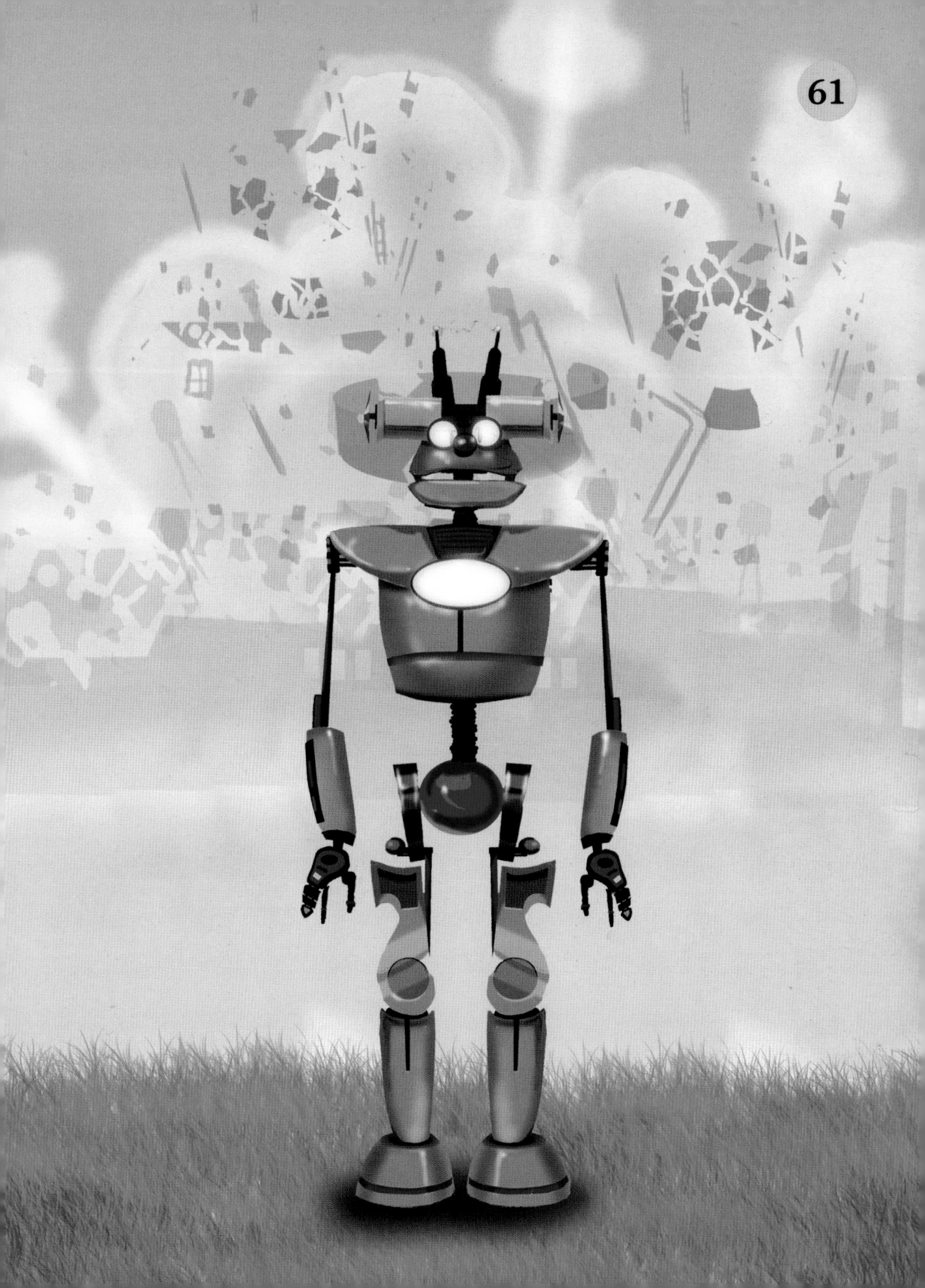

You just manage to grasp Gus's feet before he takes off, out the Emergency Exit door, and into the sky. You hear a whir, and a rubbery plastic clip secures your hands to Gus's feet.

"That's a new feature I've been working on," Gus shouts proudly. "Hand holders, so you don't fall off."

"Whoa!" Schuyler hollers. "We must be a thousand feet up!"

You look down. Everything is toy-sized. You recognize your school and the shopping center and downtown. Some people stop to stare and point as you fly by.

Suddenly you are diving down fast. Before you even have a chance to yell out, Gus has landed in your backyard.

"Phew!" Schuyler says, standing up, brushing off some grass.

Go on to the next page.

"Everybody okay?" Gus asks.

You look up as your mom comes out on the back porch.

"Oh, hi kids, hi Gus," she says. "I was wondering where you were. Anyone for some lemonade?"

The End

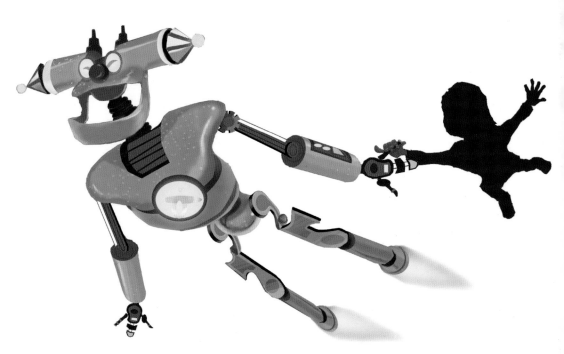

You follow Schuyler down some stairs into the basement. She leads you through a maze of hundreds of pipes. You come up on the other side into a huge two-story room.

"The Plant Manager told my mom that they shut down wastewater processing until they find Gus, which means the pipes will be empty," Schuyler says. "We can enter the pipes here or by the entrance closer to the computer room."

You take one more look at the map.

"All I know is that we have to find him before my parents find out, or they're going to make me throw Gus out in the garbage," you say.

If you decide to enter the pipes nearby, turn to page 66.

If you decide to use the entrance closer to the computer room where you know Gus was earlier, turn to page 26.

"Let's try the pipe entrance right here," you tell Schuyler.

You climb a narrow metal ladder to the top of the lowest pipe, open the hatch door and drop inside. It's dark inside the pipe. There's an inch of water, but it's not too bad. Schuyler flicks on a flashlight. You notice your footsteps make an echoing sound.

"Gus?" you say in your loudest whisper. "Are you there?"

No answer.

"Let's go this way, toward the processing area," Schuyler suggests. "That's probably the way Gus would go."

You and Schuyler walk along inside the big pipe. Your steps make little sloshing noises.

"Gus?" you whisper every few feet. But no one answers. You hear a faint rushing sound.

"What's that?" you ask Schuyler.

Turn to page 69.

The sound is getting louder.

"I think it's the…" Schuyler begins.

The water around your feet is suddenly an inch, then three inches, then twelve inches deep. Uh-oh.

"RUN FOR IT!" Schuyler screams.

First Schuyler trips and falls. Then you do.

"HEELLLLP!" you both yell.

The rushing water carries you and Schuyler along, down, underwater, then up, before it dumps you out into…

Turn to page 70.

…a HUGE lagoon.

The lagoon is filled with green plants. The lagoon is enclosed in walls and a roof of clear glass. It actually smells good, more like a greenhouse.

The sun filters down through the glass roof.

"Where are we?" you ask Schuyler as you bob along.

"You're in the Processing Lagoon, where all the city's wastewater comes for its final cleaning," Gus says. "I think it's a great day for a swim, don't you?"

"Gus!" you both exclaim.

The End

ABOUT THE ILLUSTRATOR

Illustrator Keith Newton began his art career in the theater as a set painter. Having talent and a strong desire to paint portraits, he moved to New York and studied fine art at the Art Students League. Keith has won numerous awards in art such as The Grumbacher Gold Medallion and Salmagundi Award for Pastel. He soon began illustrating and was hired by Walt Disney Feature Animation where he worked on such films as *Pocahontas* and *Mulan* as a background artist. Keith also designed color models for sculptures at Disney's Animal Kingdom and has animated commercials for Euro Disney. Today, Keith Newton freelances from his home and teaches entertainment illustration at the College for Creative Studies in Detroit. He is married and has two daughters.

ABOUT THE AUTHOR

SHANNON GILLIGAN is a writer and interactive game designer. She has spoken around the world about interface design. She lives in Warren, Vermont, with her extended family and currently wears the hat of publisher in the re-launch of *Choose Your Own Adventure*. She still hasn't written a cookbook.

R. A. Montgomery attended Hopkins Grammar School, Williston-Northhampton School and Williams College where he graduated in 1958. He pursued graduate studies in Religion and Economics at Yale and NYU. Montgomery was an adventurer all his life, climbing mountains in the Himalaya, skiing throughout Europe and scuba-diving wherever he could. His interests included education, macro-economics, geo-politics, mythology, history, mystery novels and music. He wrote his first interactive book, *Journey Under the Sea*, in 1976 and published it under the series name *The Adventures of You*. A few years later Bantam Books bought this book and gave Montgomery a contract for five more, to inaugurate their new children's publishing division. Bantam renamed the series *Choose Your Own Adventure* and a publishing phenomenon was born. The series has sold more than 260 million copies in over 40 languages. He was married to the writer Shannon Gilligan. Montgomery died in November 2014, only two months after his last book was published.

For games, activities and other fun stuff, or to write to Chooseco and Shannon Gilligan, visit us online at www.cyoa.com

Watch for these titles coming up in the

CHOOSE YOUR OWN ADVENTURE®

Dragonlarks® series for Beginning Readers

Always Picked Last • Your Very Own Robot Goes Cuckoo-Bananas • Return to
Haunted House • The Owl Tree • The Lake Monster Mystery • Your Very Own Robot
The Haunted House • Your Purrr-fect Birthday • Sand Castle • Ghost Island • Caravan
Space Pup • Gus Vs. The Robot King • Lost Dog • Your Grandparents Are Zombies
Dragon Day • Search for the Dragon Queen • Monsters of the Deep • Indian Trail

 Purchase online at www.cyoa.com or ask your local bookseller